Barbara ♡.
I hope you enjoy
reading the story to
your grandchildren ...
Wishing you
Lots of Love &
Joy in your
life :"
Wendy F.F.

MW00954675

1/2/20

ZZ Black

By Wendy Plumb

With Illustrations by
Xavier Pom

WALDORF PUBLISHING

Published by Waldorf Publishing
2140 Hall Johnson Road
#102-345
Grapevine, Texas 76051
www.WaldorfPublishing.com

ZZ Black: The classic tale of a girl and the horse she loved

ISBN: 978-1-64136-843-8
Library of Congress Control Number: 2018933249

I dedicate this book to my daughter, Vienna, who I love with all my heart and who has taught me to believe.

And to Z, who inspired me to dream.

"ZZ Black is an extraordinary tale of love. Sometimes all you need is that one person to believe in you and then anything is possible!"

> Dylan McDermott,
> Actor and father father of 2 girls.

"ZZ Black is a beautiful lesson. It teaches children to think of others. I loved reading this special book to our twins."

> Neil Jacobson,
> President at Geffen Records and father of twins.

Table of Contents

Kate Dreams of a Horse 1

The Wild Stallion 8

Black on the Mountaintop 12

Trouble at the Farm 18

Bargaining for Black 21

Learning to Speak 26

Kate Makes a Plan 31

Courage and Forgiveness 35

Chapter 1
Kate Dreams of a Horse

In the early moments of dawn, thick fog clung to the trees as the sun gathered its strength to shine down upon Whispering Farm. Kate was wrapped tightly inside her blankets like a caterpillar in a cocoon. As she slowly awakened, she remembered it was Saturday. Kate loved Saturdays – it was her favorite day of the week. She had no school and could spend all of her time with the animals on the farm.

"Ahhhh," she sighed loudly, stretching her arms into the air. Pebbles, her golden retriever, jumped up onto the bed and began licking her face. Kate laughed at the soft, wet sensation. "Good morning, Pebbles. Guess what?" she asked.

"What?" Pebbles replied in the deep, rumbling voice Kate had loved ever since she was small.

"I got my report card yesterday," she announced.

Kate had made a deal with her father that if she got straight A's he would allow her to get a horse. Kate wanted nothing more than a horse of her own.

She jumped out of bed and shuffled through her backpack. "Look!" she said proudly, holding up the slip of paper.

"Wow!" said Pebbles, wagging his golden tail.

"I can't wait to find Dad and tell him the good news."

Full of excitement, Kate hurried to get dressed. She could smell the coffee from downstairs and the wood smoke from the stove. Kate's father, Mr. Whitmore, always rose before sunrise. He would make Kate fresh biscuits and leave them warm in the oven. Saturday morning was their special time together. They would stroll the farm side by side and Mr. Whitmore would share with her everything she missed while she was studying at school that week. Kate admired her father's hard work ethic and loyalty to the farm. Even though he was a busy man he never missed his mornings with Kate. It meant a lot to both of them.

Kate sprinted down the stairs with Pebbles following at her heels. She could hardly wait to find her father.

Shoving her feet into her rubber boots, Kate pushed open the side door and stepped into the country morning air. The grass was wet and the ground still damp. Flowers were blooming; spring was coming soon.

On the way to the stables Kate and Pebbles stopped to say hello to Maverick, the rooster, who was pacing back and forth in front of the barn. The barn, bright red with white trim, was special – it was magical. Ever since Kate was a little girl she knew it allowed the animals who lived inside it to talk.

"Hello, Maverick!" Kate yelled out. "How are you?"

"Very well," replied the rooster. And then they both exclaimed at the same time: "Good news!"

Laughing, Kate told Maverick, "You go first."

The proud rooster cleared his throat. "Myra's eggs hatched today. Five baby chicks were born!"

Kate gasped with delight. "That's wonderful – you're a dad now!"

"It's a big responsibility," Maverick admitted. "I'm not used to watching over them yet. I have to do everything I can to keep them safe."

Kate knew the rooster's words were important, but her head was still bubbling over with the news of her report card. "I'm on my way to find my father," she gushed. "I got straight A's!"

"Congratulations!" said Maverick. "Does this mean you'll finally get your own horse?"

"Yes, it certainly does," she replied with a confident grin.

"We'll be back to see Myra and the chicks as soon we find my dad to tell him the great news. Let's go, Pebbles," Kate called, hurrying off.

***

Mr. Whitmore was hard at work cleaning up the pastures when Kate crept up and surprised him from behind. "Boo!" she said, giving him a big hug. She proudly handed him her report card.

"You definitely earned a horse, young lady," he said, looking it over. "I'm proud of you, Kate. I knew you could do it."

Kate beamed.

"Now hurry off, I need to get back to work. There's a herd of horses arriving today, and these pastures need to be groomed," her father said.

"A herd of horses?" Kate asked cautiously, her ears perking up.

"Easy does it, young lady," said her father. "We'll find you a horse, but not today. The horses coming today are future polo horses. They need to be trained and sold. Go on now..."

Ignoring her father's words, Kate squealed with anticipation. "Did you hear that, Pebbles? Let's tell Maverick and the others about the horses arriving today."

As they walked back to the red barn, Kate asked Pebbles, "Do you think it's possible that there's a horse for me in that herd?"

"Anything's possible," Pebbles replied. "You've held onto this dream for a long time and worked hard to earn it. There's no reason why it can't come true."

"You're right, Pebbles!"

When they got back to the barn and shared the news, Maverick immediately flew into a frenzy of clucking and feathers. "I need to get the barn tidied up and make sure the chicks stay out of the way. You know your father – when new horses arrive, it means business. Nothing should be in the way," he said in a slight panic.

"Stuart can help clean up," Pebbles suggested, thinking of the elderly pig, the barn's senior resident. "It will give him something to do."

"Good idea, Pebbles," said Kate.

She pushed open the barn's creaky door and stepped inside to find Myra teaching her newly hatched chicks how to walk. "Come on girls, you can do it. Keep following mama and stay in one straight line," the hen ordered sternly. Startled by Kate's presence, all of the chicks fell down and rolled out of line. Myra clucked in frustration, but seeing Kate, her face brightened with excitement. "Oh, Kate, come in, dear," she said.

Enchanted by the chicks, Kate kneeled down. "Lean closer, dear, they'll want to see your face," Myra urged. "This is Lilly, Lulu, Lizzie, Liza and Luella," she announced, introducing them one by one.

"Welcome to the world," said Kate in a whisper.

Everyone gathered close as Kate shared the news of the day. Even Stuart stood up from his cozy corner, not wanting to be left out.

But all she could really think about was her mystery horse.

Chapter 2
The Wild Stallion

All at once, a roaring vibration came from down the road. The ground began to shake as the sound grew closer. Everyone in the barn exchanged glances. Pebbles bounded toward the open window. Kate sprang up to follow.

Seconds later, two big horse trailers appeared and pulled up close to the barn. As the first trailer stopped, a voice cried out from behind the wheel. "Howdy!"

"It's the horses!" Kate told the others.

She watched closely as her father strode over to meet the farmer. Then she slowly moved away from the window, stepped out of the barn and crept quietly out toward the trailers, her curiosity too strong to suppress.

"In the first trailer you got the two mares and a filly; in the second you'll find the stallions," she heard the driver say to her father.

There was always something about horses that made Kate's heart soar. Even as a little girl, when everyone would be off at the fair, Kate would vanish into the stalls, finding refuge among the horses' silky manes and soulful eyes.

But as much as Mr. Whitmore enjoyed watching his daughter's excitement, to him today was all business.

"Just a minute, young lady," he ordered, holding up his hand to stop her from getting too close. "Let's get these horses up to the pasture and let them out to run."

As the trailers pulled forward, Kate noticed a third trailer rumbling toward the barn. "Who's that?" she asked, pointing down the road.

"I don't know," replied her father. He squinted to get a better look at what was coming.

A smaller trailer rolled up and pulled to a stop in the dirt. Kate could see that it was carrying only one horse.

"What can we do for you?" Mr. Whitmore asked, ambling up to the truck's window.

"I'm just passing through, waiting for my boy to drop off your horses," the bearded driver answered with a friendly smile. "Then I'm heading up to Carla's Pass with my passenger here."

Suddenly a thunderous boom sounded from within the trailer and everyone froze.

Boom. Boom. Boom. It was coming from the back of the trailer. The horse was kicking the walls from the inside and neighing at the top of his lungs. The fierce display captured everyone's attention, but before Mr. Whitmore could react, the back door of the trailer exploded open and a towering black horse bolted out like lightning from a storm.

At full speed, the horse charged toward the barn. Clods of dirt flew everywhere.

Everyone stood shocked.

"Watch out!" yelled the farmer, as the horse tried jumping the fence. He barely made it over the top, splitting the wood in two with a loud crack.

"That horse is out of control!" cried Maverick, slamming the gate so the horse couldn't get in.

"Hold on!" screamed Myra to the chicks as they went flying into the air in a nervous, fluffy jumble. Stuart tried to catch them. "I gotcha!" he yelled as they landed with a sticky splat in his pile of manure.

Chaos erupted everywhere the horse turned.

The horse didn't know what to do or which way to go. He was frightened, so he kept on running.

Mr. Whitmore grabbed the lead rope and halter from the back of the truck. The horse finally stopped, unsure of where to go next.

Without fear, Kate began walking toward the now-still horse. "Who is this horse?" she wondered aloud.

"Careful, Kate," warned her father. "Move slowly."

"It's okay, boy. Nobody's going to hurt you," she murmured as she approached. To her father, she said, "Give me the halter."

Kate was nearly in front of the big, black horse. "Steady, boy," she said.

At that moment the horse, which had never been tamed, was calm in her presence. The two of them stood face to face, staring into each other's eyes.

Mr. Whitmore hesitated before handing his daughter the halter.

To everyone's amazement, the powerful horse stood still and let Kate slip the halter over his jaw.

"Watch your daughter with that crazy stallion," shouted the farmer. "He's a wild one. In fact, I'm surprised she got him to calm down at all. No one can usually get near Black – he's as hard-headed as horses can be. Too much abuse in his earlier years... Yeah, a real shame. Good looking horse, too, and strong as one can be."

Mr. Whitmore listened to what the man was saying as he watched his daughter with the horse. It was true: He was an exceptional-looking horse – strong and dark, a shade of black close to midnight. He was fierce; anyone could see that a mile away. Black had something that Kate's father knew from years of experience was rare. He just wasn't sure he wanted his only daughter getting involved with an animal that unpredictable.

Kate looked at her father. She could see he was concerned. "Oh, Daddy," she pleaded gently, "Can I have him? Please, can I have him?"

Chapter 3
Black on the Mountaintop

ZZ Black was his full name, but they called him Black for short. He was sleek and dark with deep-set eyes. As a colt he was sent to a farm where he was badly mistreated. Black was ignored and beaten by his owners, who didn't care about him once it was decided that he wouldn't be a racehorse. He became reclusive and angry. All he thought about was running away and never being found. Once, Black managed to escape, but he was captured by a group of farmers who sent him right back to the place he disliked so much.

Being an exceptionally strong and good looking horse, he was eventually purchased for a small price. Yet despite his new surroundings, his spirit never seemed to settle. He had a gentle heart, but his temper was quick and fierce. Most people misunderstood Black. They didn't see the kind core in him, only the wild. Black felt afraid and constantly alone, until the day he met Kate. He trusted her. It was as though they had known each other for many lifetimes.

Every free moment Kate had, she spent with Black. They loved being together. She would wash him until he was shiny clean, feed him until his belly was full and read to him in the orchard under the apple tree.

For the first time ever, Black felt happy and his spirits began to lift.

Mr. Whitmore had been reluctant to let Black stay, but Kate earned her horse and he couldn't say no. Kate's unwavering spirit reminded him of her mother's – she would fight bravely for what she held dear. It was time to let Kate experience what it was like to care for a horse, even if that horse was as reckless as Black.

***

"Come on Black, let's go!" said Kate as they galloped off into woods one afternoon. "I have a special place to show you. It's at the top of that hill. I think you're going to love it!" She guided Black toward the hillside and goaded him onward.

After riding for over an hour, they finally reached the top of the hill. From there, they could see rolling mountains that went on for miles. Horses grazed freely among the leafy trees below.

"That's one of the most beautiful views I've ever seen," Kate mused wistfully, gazing out over the valley and the mountain range beyond. "I wish we could ride forever."

Black just stared. He was absolutely still. Not a sound. Not a whisper.

"I brought your favorite, carrots," Kate offered. Black didn't seem to notice. He simply gazed out over the vast terrain.

"What's wrong, boy? Are you okay?" she asked, patting his back.

Black saw something, something he remembered from a long time ago. He was mesmerized.

Just then, the wind started to blow. The leaves rustled and the branches shook and Black kicked his legs high into the air.

"Whoa, boy! What's gotten into you?" Kate asked, jumping out of his way. The beautiful, strong horse yanked his head back and neighed loudly into the open air. His restless spirit was trying to say something, but she didn't know what.

"Come on, Black, let's head back," she said. "It's getting late and I'm sure everyone will be worried by now." As she jumped onto his back, the wind whistled louder and the leaves shook harder. Black began to run. He ran faster and faster and faster! Kate closed her eyes and held on tight as the wind whipped her hair.

When she opened her eyes they were home. The barn was bathed in bright moonlight. She breathed a sigh of relief as she dismounted, and led Black up the path toward the stables.

"Shhh," Kate whispered as they tiptoed into the barn. "We don't want anyone to hear us."

Just then a voice called out, "Kate, where have you been?" Pebbles stood in the shadow of the open door.

"Oh, Pebbles, you scared me!" gasped Kate.

"You know it's not safe to be out there in those mountains after dark."

"I know," Kate admitted, looking down at Pebbles sheepishly. "I'm sorry, we just lost track of time."

Kate felt bad; she knew Pebbles was right. If her father found out he would take Black away and she would be grounded forever.

"Say goodnight and I'll wait for you near the house. I left the side door open so you could sneak through," he told her.

"Thank you!" she sighed. Turning to Black, she added, "Come on, boy. Let's go get you some water. I bet you're thirsty."

Kate walked Black into his stall. She filled his bucket of water, then sat down and watched him pensively for a long time.

"I'm going to have to go for now," she said, brushing him down. "I have to get back to the house before Dad comes looking for me. I don't want us getting into any more trouble tonight."

Black whined sadly.

"What's wrong, boy? I'll be back in the morning," she said softly. Still, she could tell that there was something else troubling him.

"You saw something out there on that hilltop, didn't you?" she asked.

Black wished he could tell her, but he didn't know how.

Kate sighed. "Good night," she said, kissing his forehead. She quietly walked back to the house.

Pebbles was waiting for her at the side door. "Let's get to bed," he said with a drowsy yawn. Kate could tell he was disappointed in her, but she didn't know how to fix it. As she lay awake, she remembered Black's frenzied neighing and his taut muscles as he raced down the hill, headlong into the icy wind.

Chapter 4
Trouble at the Farm

While the other horses slept, Black stood awake. He was cold and lonely. He thought of Kate. He thought of the mountaintop. He struggled.

Kate rushed off to school early the next morning and didn't have a chance to say goodbye. The day seemed endless, and Black grew anxious. When the farmer came by for a feeding Black nearly bit his head right off.

"What in the world is wrong with you?" yelled the farmer. "You crazy horse!"

Black kicked and kicked, harder and harder until the farmer left, muttering to himself. The other horses got excited. They started kicking in their stalls too. Once again Black sent the farm into chaos.

Maverick and Myra could hear the loud racket coming from the horse stalls down at the red barn. "Is that poor Black making all of that noise?" asked Myra, sheltering her chicks from the din.

"It certainly is!" replied Maverick. He paced back and forth by the barn window, casting worried glances outside.

"Maybe you should go play with him, dear. He needs a friend. He's awfully frustrated when Kate's not around," Myra suggested.

"Play with him? I'm not going to play with him!" Maverick replied, puffing out his chest. "I'm not going near that horse. He's wild and he's bad news. I haven't the faintest idea why Kate spends so much time with him. It's a real waste as far as I'm concerned, a waste indeed," continued Maverick as he shuffled across the barn.

"Well I, for one, feel sorry for him. He's suffering and we don't know why," Myra said gently. "I wonder why he hasn't said anything since he's gotten here."

"I think he's cute!" said Lilly, giggling with the other chicks.

"None of that nonsense coming from you girls!" Maverick crowed. "You stay away from that horse – he's no good for you."

"Don't be such a pessimist," Stuart piped up from his stack of hay. "Everyone needs a little loving and looking out for."

At that moment, a loud rumble issued from the stalls. Everyone froze.

"You hear all that excitement? That horse doesn't need love – he needs discipline!" Maverick shouted.

"Look!" Pebbles pointed outside. "Mr. Whitmore is taking Black somewhere."

They all crowded around the barn window. Black was being led out of the stables. He did not look happy. "Where do you think he's taking him?" asked Myra.

Everyone exchanged concerned glances.

***

When Kate got home from school, Black was gone. She looked everywhere. Frantic, she ran out of his empty stall and went to find her father. She found him working in the pasture with the other horses.

"Dad, Dad," she cried out. "Black is missing! Where did he go?"

"Calm down, Kate!" her father said. He wiped the sweat from his forehead.

"Calm down?" Kate yelled. "My horse is gone! How can you tell me to calm down?"

Tears rolled down her cheeks. She didn't know what to do.

"Kate, please listen," said Mr. Whitmore. "You have to trust me. I know more about horses than you do. That horse of yours needs special training. I sent him to Mr. Peters' farm to have a looking at. Don't worry, he'll be back."

"But that's unfair," Kate protested. "He's my horse and you didn't ask me first. I spend the most time with him and I know what's best for him."

"I know you may think you do, Kate, but you're only twelve years old. You took on a great responsibility taking care of Black, but he's no ordinary horse. If he keeps behaving this way he's going to cause havoc everywhere."

"But I love him no matter what!" Kate could barely get the words out.

"Of course you do, but love can't teach a horse to behave. He's liable to hurt some-one – even you." Mr. Whitmore felt bad. He could see how much pain Kate was in, but he knew she'd have to learn this lesson sooner or later. "Go on back to the house now. I'm sure you've got some studying to do."

The last thing Kate wanted to do was homework. *What is Black thinking now?* she wondered. *Does he think I gave him up?* The thought made her sob all over again.

Chapter 5
Bargaining for Black

The next day was rainy and dark. Kate hoped the sun would shine, but it hid stubbornly behind a thick cover of clouds. Black was returning today, but the weather didn't seem cheerful at all. She knew how scared he probably felt without her.

"Pebbles, do you think Black is happy here?" Kate asked, staring out her bedroom window. "I love him so much. I want him to be happy."

Pebbles saw the tears running down her face. He chose his words carefully. "Well... no matter how much you love someone, you can't will them to be happy. But it would help if you knew *why* he was unhappy."

"That's true," she said, wiping her tears with her sleeve. "I have to figure out what's making him act out like this. Even the other day, when we rode to the top of the hill, he was acting strange – almost like he saw a ghost."

"Hmm," Pebbles mused. "Did you ask him what he saw?"

"I tried, but he doesn't talk," said Kate sadly.

"He doesn't talk? That's strange."

"Nope, not a word. He doesn't seem to want to."

"Maybe he can't. Or maybe he's scared to," Pebbles said thoughtfully.

"If I could just get him to talk…" Kate trailed off, deep in thought. Just then an idea came to her. "Maybe there is a way to get Black to talk, after all: the barn! We need to get him inside the barn, where everyone else talks. Maybe that will encourage him."

"Great idea, Kate! The magic of the red barn will certainly get him to talk," replied Pebbles.

Kate barely noticed the rain as she took off running toward the stables, eager for Black's return. But as she approached, she could hear a racket inside. "Oh no," she thought to herself. "Not again."

Sure enough, she arrived to find chaos. All of the horses were kicking their legs in the air and banging on the stall walls, neighing and gnashing their teeth. Black had just gotten back, and he was already stirring up trouble.

"You need to tame that horse of yours once and for all!" shouted the farmer, holding back one of the other horses. "He's made a real mess of the place!"

Kate walked in and could see the stables were in shambles. She went directly up to Black and looked him straight in the eyes. "What are you doing, boy?" she asked in a gentle voice.

There was a deep scratch above his right eye and a rivulet of blood dripped down his face. His mane was tangled in knots. He looked at her fearfully and lowered his head.

"If you keep acting this way you're going to get us both in a lot of trouble," she said, petting the top of his head. She knew she should be stern with him, but one look at his deep, soulful eyes and her resolve broke.

Black looked down, ashamed. He knew he didn't deserve Kate's kindness after what he'd done.

"It's okay, boy," Kate said. "I know you're sorry but we need to figure out why you keep misbehaving. When the rain stops I'm going to take you down to the red barn. In the barn, everyone talks. I believe you can talk, too."

Black continued to watch Kate as she wiped away the blood from his face, brushed his tail and got to work cleaning up his mess. He felt calm again knowing she was near.

The rain came down hard, beating rhythmically on the roof of the stable. Kate was tired. She snuggled down in the hay next to Black and fell asleep at his side.

***

Hours passed. Kate was awakened by beams of late-afternoon sunlight peeking through the cracks of the wooden stable walls. When she opened her eyes, Mr. Whitmore was standing above her. His mouth was set in a grim line.

"What time is it?" she asked, still groggy.

"It's time for you to get yourself up," her father said.

Kate stood up and brushed the dusty hay off of her jeans. "The rain stopped," she said brightly.

"Why don't you go out and play with the other kids instead of spending all your time here in the barn, Kate?"

Black stood near, listening.

"I don't want to play with the other kids," Kate replied in a stubborn voice. "I want to be with Black. Besides, I'm going to teach him to talk so we can find out what's wrong with him. Then you won't have to take him away."

Her father looked concerned. "Kate, there you go inventing things again. You know horses don't talk! That's the silliest thing I've ever heard. And even if he could talk, what makes you think that will make him behave? I know you care about him, but he needs something you can't possibly give him. You're a young girl who should not be worrying about a damaged wild horse."

"Damaged? He's not damaged! He just needs someone to love him." Kate looked at her father like she'd never looked at him before.

"I don't think you understand, Kate."

"Understand what?" she said as took the saddle from its peg on the wall.

"Understand that this horse is going to have to go."

Black became anxious. He could tell what was being said.

"Just get rid of him? Send him to a place where nobody cares?" Kate cried. "I won't let you!" Kate threw her arms around Black and clung to his thick, dark mane.

"Listen here, Kate," said her father. "This horse is bound to hurt someone cooped up in here like this. He's just not fit for this kind of living."

Kate didn't want to hear what her father had to say, even though deep down inside she knew he might be right.

Kate knew she had get Black to talk soon. If she didn't, there might not be a chance to save him.

Chapter 6
Learning to Speak

Pebbles raced down to the red barn as fast as his paws could carry him. In a breathless voice, he announced to the others Kate's plan to bring Black to the barn. "She believes that if she can get him inside the barn he will try to talk," Pebbles explained.

"That's a wonderful idea," Myra said. "Kate would be so pleased to hear him talk."

"Why can't he talk?" asked one of the little chicks.

"Probably because he never believed he could," Pebbles replied in a tender voice.

"Do you have to believe you can talk?" asked another chick.

"Anything you want to do that you can't already do, you must first believe you can."

"I don't believe he can," Maverick called out from his perch high atop the fence. "And even if he could, why should we care what he has to say, anyway?"

"Oh, Maverick, that's a hopeless way to think," scolded Myra. "You never know what you might learn from someone just by listening to them."

"We have to give him a chance," said Pebbles. "Everyone deserves a chance."

"He can do it!" Stuart piped up. "If one thing is for sure, he loves Kate. If he can talk, he will."

"I'm not so sure about that," Maverick argued. "If he loves her so much, why does he behave so badly when she's not around? He's making trouble for them both."

"That's what she intends to find out. And we must help her do so," said Pebbles.

"In other words, you're going to keep your big beak shut!" Myra commanded, glaring up at Maverick.

"So we all agree that when they arrive, we will do everything we can to help Black *believe*," proposed Pebbles.

"We believe!" all five chicks exclaimed together.

Moments later, from his perch on top of the fence, Maverick could see Kate riding Black up the path toward the barn. "Here they come," he announced loudly. Myra scrambled to put her chicks in a neat row. Stuart stood up from his bale of hay and shook himself off. Everyone looked toward the barn door in anticipation.

Meanwhile, as Kate rode Black up the dirt road she tried to prepare him for the task ahead.

"When we go into the barn you'll see how easy it will be to talk," she explained in an encouraging manner. "All of the animals in the red barn talk, so don't be embarrassed or shy."

Black felt apprehensive. What if he couldn't talk like everyone else?

Kate waved to Maverick as they approached the barn. There was an expectant stillness in the air. "Hello, Maverick!" she called out.

Black and Maverick stared at one another for a tense moment. Respectfully, Maverick nodded his head and welcomed Black through the gate and into the barn. Typically fierce and stubborn, Black began to feel a gentleness roll through his body. For the first time he felt vulnerable.

Kate jumped down off of his back and led Black through the barn door slowly. "Don't be afraid," she whispered. "Everybody here is your friend."

The five chicks sat side by side in awe looking up at the big black stallion. They were at a loss for words; they didn't even peep. "Welcome," said Myra in a gentle, warm tone. Even she was a little bit intimidated by the presence of the tall, dark animal.

Black looked around. The barn was small. It smelled mostly of hay but not the hay from the horse stall. It was golden and warm and made Black feel peaceful.

"Come in a little closer," said Stuart. "There's plenty of room in here for you."

Black took one step followed by another. For a moment he wavered and felt like running away. It was all so different, so strange. But something deep down wouldn't let him turn around. He felt safe. He took a deep breath. Everyone was sitting quietly, facing Black. Even Maverick didn't say a word.

Suddenly a magical light came shining down through the ceiling of the barn. The entire barn lit up. Then the light softened into a gentle glow, which settled around Black and Black alone.

Kate peered anxiously at Black and held her breath.

Black lifted his face. Finally, he felt ready to use his voice. "Thank you," he sighed, looking up at Kate.

Kate grinned and stroked his long face happily. "Thank *you*," she replied, laughing with relief. "Thank you for finding the courage to talk."

"Courage?" he asked.

"It takes courage to do something you've never done before," she said.

"And to believe in yourself," cried out one of the chicks, excited to have witnessed this surprising occasion.

"And let's not also forget love," added Myra, leaning her head toward Maverick's.

"Which is the magic you feel in this barn," Kate finished.

Black hesitated. He looked nervously at Kate.

"Is there something you want to say?" she asked him.

"I love you very much, and I wish I could stay with you forever," Black began. Kate tensed up. She could tell he was going to say something she didn't want to hear.

"I want to stay with you forever, too," she replied, tentatively.

"When I'm with you, it almost feels like home," Black went on. "It's just that... I think my real home is somewhere else. Somewhere without walls and fences, out among the fields and trees."

Tears welled up in Kate's eyes as she listened to the proud horse searching for words.

"Will you still love me if I tell you I need to be set free?"

Kate couldn't hold back her sobs anymore. In that moment she knew deep down that she had to let him go. No matter how much she loved him she couldn't protect him from the life he had to lead.

"I wish I could be the horse you want me to be, but I'm a horse that needs to be out in the wild world," Black continued as a tear rolled down his face. "Otherwise I don't know who I am."

Kate knew what she should tell Black; she knew what she needed to say to comfort him. But it was too much for her just then, too hard to get the words out. She had so hoped that she could fix him so she could keep him by her side. What would she do without him?

Chapter 7
Kate Makes a Plan

That night Kate barely slept. She tossed and turned until she finally gave up on sleeping at all. Could she really give up her horse – the horse she had dreamed of all her life? "What did I do wrong?" she kept thinking. "Did I not love him enough?" Yet she knew that couldn't be true because she had never loved anyone so much.

Kate was terribly confused. She loved being needed by Black. It made her feel special knowing she was the only one who made him happy. It never occurred to her that one day he would want to leave. "Maybe if I ride him more he'll feel freer, or I could make him a bigger stall so he has more room?" Kate wondered. "There has to be something I can do so he'll be happier."

Leaning out her bedroom window, Kate looked up at the star-filled sky.

"Please help me know what to do," she begged. She wished on every star she saw that she might find a way to keep Black close to her. She couldn't bear life without him. Somehow she would have to find a way.

Exhausted from thinking so much, she curled up on the carpet, closed her eyes and fell asleep. She dreamed of a shooting star bursting through the northern sky. She and Black were standing on top of a high, majestic peak, and together they could touch the stars.

The next morning Kate awoke groggily and went downstairs to the kitchen for a glass of milk. As she opened the refrigerator door she heard her father's muffled voice coming from down the hallway. He was on the phone. She tiptoed closer to his office door so she could listen to what was going on.

"That sounds good, Peters, I'll be here," he said. "It's not going to be easy getting that horse harnessed and willing to go, but I'll talk to Kate and make sure she understands what has to be done."

Kate gasped and then covered her mouth quickly. She couldn't believe her ears. Was her father really going to have Black taken away to another farm? That was the last thing he needed! Leaning back against the kitchen wall, she felt paralyzed. "Take a deep breath," she told herself. "No one is taking Black away – not if I can help it!"

Her father hung up the phone; Kate could hear him heading toward the kitchen. Frantically, she slid in her socks across the wooden floor back to the refrigerator. She reached for the carton of milk as though she hadn't heard a thing.

When her father walked into the kitchen he was surprised to see her. "Good morning," he said, appearing to steel himself for an unpleasant conversation.

"Good morning," Kate replied, not turning around as she poured her milk.

"I'm running into town to pick up a few things – do you want to come with me?"

"No thanks, I have studying to do here," Kate said nonchalantly.

Her father paused. "Mr. Peters is coming in a couple of hours," he began tentatively.

"Oh, really? Why is that?" Kate asked, her heart pounding.

"He found a suitable farm for Black. Somewhere he'll be happier, perfect for his type of temperament."

Kate's stomach dropped at these words but she kept her cool.

"He wants to talk it over with you before taking him, of course."

"When did you say he was coming?" she asked, looking up at clock over the kitchen sink.

"Sometime around 3 or 4 o'clock."

Kate realized she didn't have a lot of time. She had to find a way to hide Black before Mr. Peters arrived – otherwise she wouldn't have a chance to save him.

"I know it's hard giving up that horse, but in time you'll see this was the right decision. He'll be in a much better place and happier in the long run," her father continued gently. "And honey, don't you worry, we'll find you another horse soon. I promise."

Suffocated by his words, Kate scrambled to reach the kitchen door.

"I'm going to feed the animals now," she called as she stumbled outside. The door swung shut and closed behind her.

***

Outside the house, Kate paused and took a long, deep breath. She looked out toward the barn as she gathered her thoughts. *How can I hide Black? Where can I take him?* she wondered.

Suddenly she remembered her dream from last night: standing on top of the mountain, reaching for the midnight stars. The dream had carried a feeling of lightness and freedom. *Freedom*, she thought. *That's what Black wanted.* "That's it!" she said aloud. "I'm going to take Black to the mountaintop where we saw those wild horses and from there, I'll let him run free." Kate felt an immediate sense of relief. In fact, she was surprised by the sudden surge of energy she felt when she imagined giving her beloved horse the one gift he truly wanted.

As Kate's father pulled away in his truck, she waved goodbye. Then she rushed over to the red barn to find Pebbles.

"Pebbles!" she shouted, and then spotted him sniffing diligently through some greenish shrubs. He instantly looked up and ran toward Kate. As he jumped up to lick her face, he could tell she had something on her mind.

"I need your help," she began, launching into her plan to steal Black away and release him on the mountaintop. "If I don't let him go this way, Mr. Peters is going to take him to another fenced-in place where he'll be miserable and unhappy. I can't let that happen to him," she pleaded desperately.

Pebbles listened. He knew she was scared but he also knew she was determined. Nothing was going to change her mind. "How can I help?" he asked.

"It's going to take me some time to get to the mountain range and I'm not even sure how I'm going to return," Kate said. "My father is sure to come looking for me. I need you to distract him in any way you can, at least until I get there."

"Are you sure you want to do this, Kate?" Pebbles cautioned.

"Yes!" she replied without a trace of doubt. "There is no other choice!"

Chapter 8
Courage and Forgiveness

Kate ran to the stables with Pebbles bounding closely behind. When she arrived, she found Black standing in his stall with his head pointed outward over the top of the door. He was waiting for Kate, and he was anxious.

"Hello, boy!" she called, forcing her voice to be uplifting and bright. But she couldn't keep up the act. This would be the last time she would see him in his stall, after all.

Kate opened the stall door and grabbed the leather harness from the wall. "We're going to go on a ride," she announced sadly but with a smile. Black lowered his head dutifully, but flicked his tail in apprehension. Why was Kate so tense?

She led him out of the stall and then jumped up on his back. Black, still unsure where they were going, didn't say a word. Pebbles had been waiting patiently outside the stall; he looked up at Black and said a silent goodbye. He felt a little melancholy in his heart. Despite all of the trouble the big black horse caused, he would miss the animal's presence and how happy he made Kate.

"I guess this is it," Kate said. Pebbles could hear in her voice that she was nervous. "You ready to go for a ride, boy?" she asked, petting his long, black mane. No one said a word. There was a moment of peace among the three, as if time stood still. Even the birds seemed to stop flying in the air. None of them knew what to do or say next.

Finally, breaking the silence, Black replied softly, "Only if you are." In that second Kate became fully aware it was time for her to take the reins. There was no option of turning back. She made her decision.

"Then let's go," she said bravely. And off they rode.

Pebbles ran behind them as they galloped off toward the forest, leaving the stables of Whispering Farm behind. Eventually Pebbles slowed his gait as he grew short of breath. The horse's flying black tail and Kate's straw-colored hair appeared to mingle as they grew smaller and smaller in the distance. Then they disappeared.

Kate and Black rode for what felt like hours. Kate could feel the horse's hooves pounding against the ground rhythmically. She could feel his heart beating hard. "We're going to the mountain top," she yelled as Black galloped headlong into the wind. Realization dawned on Black: he knew where she was taking him and they both knew it was going to be their last ride.

When they finally arrived at the top of the ridge the sun was setting beyond the distant mountains. The air was quiet and still. Only the call of a bird echoed among the pines that rolled away beneath them into the forested valley.

The big black stallion froze in his tracks, aware that this was as far as he could go with Kate. Together they gazed out into a world of uncertainty. Kate climbed off the horse's back and put her head next to his.

"I feel like I'm about to jump off a cliff," Black said, looking out at the boundless open land.

"Me too," she replied.

"You loved me like no one else ever loved me. I will never forget that."

Kate turned to him and looked into his large, dark eyes. A tear rolled down his face.

"You deserve a horse that will appreciate your kindness, your courage and your open heart – a horse that can stay by your side, that doesn't need to wander," Black continued as she wiped away the falling tear. "And will you please promise me one thing?"

"Anything," she answered.

"Don't give up on your dream. You deserve to love another horse."

Kate wrung her hands. She couldn't imagine feeling this way about another animal, but then again, she couldn't have predicted the depth of her caring for Black, either. "I promise," she finally replied. She reached out and wrapped her arms around his strong, pulsing chest and held him tight. "I will always love you."

With that, Black turned and galloped down the mountainside, his mane flying free in the wind. Kate stood at the ridge and watched him descend into the pines, now dark with twilight. She sniffled as she followed his trail with her eyes.

When she could no longer see Black she realized she was standing alone. Her day had been focused solely on setting Black free; she forgot to think about how she was going to get back home. "It's going to be a long walk," she thought to herself. But what choice did she have?

Tired and cold, Kate turned back toward the farm. But as she wound her way down the trail, she noticed a truck parked off to the side in a clearing. It was her father. Kate stopped and gasped. "Daddy!" she cried, her feet carrying her toward the truck before she could even think about it. He stood with open arms as his daughter came rushing toward him.

Kate couldn't remember needing her father more than in that moment. They held each other tightly. Kate sobbed with relief. When she caught her breath, she looked up at him and suddenly felt ashamed that she'd snuck out without telling him. "Are you mad at me?"

"No, sweetheart, I'm not mad at you," he replied.

She laid her head on his chest. "How did you find me?" she asked.

"I would have done anything to find you, Kate."

She couldn't stop hugging him.

"Let's just say you have a lot of friends who care about you living in a bright red barn," he continued with a little chuckle.

For a moment Kate said nothing. Then she realized her father must have spoken to the animals. She looked up sharply, her mouth open in shock. "You can talk to them, too?" she asked incredulously.

"What's life without a little bit of mystery?" he replied mischievously.

Kate giggled, suddenly full of stories and questions for her father. "Let's go home," she said as the truck's engine hummed to life and they started the drive back to the farm.

The End

CPSIA information can be obtained
at www.ICGtesting.com
Printed in the USA
BVHW020039210519
548827BV00003B/27/P